curve-billed thrasher  gila monster  coral snake  desert centipede  horned lizard

monarch  spadefoot toad  red-tailed hawk  desert millipede

great horned owl  javelina  mule deer

cactus mouse  mourning doves  coyote  gambel's quail  long-nosed bats  black-chinned hummingbird

# A Desert Scrapbook
## Dawn to Dusk in the Sonoran Desert

cactus wren

by Virginia Wright-Frierson

Aladdin Paperbacks

New York London Toronto
Sydney Singapore

OREGON
IDAHO
GREAT BASIN DESERT
CALIFORNIA
NEVADA
UTAH
MOJAVE DESERT
ARIZONA
SONORAN DESERT
NEW MEXICO
MEXICO
CHIHUAHUAN DESERT

First Aladdin Paperbacks edition May 2002
Copyright © 1998 Virginia Wright-Frierson

Aladdin Paperbacks
An imprint of Simon & Schuster Children's Publishing Division
1230 Avenue of the Americas New York, NY 10020

Also available in a Simon & Schuster Books for Young Readers hardcover edition.
The text of this book is set in Palantino.
The illustrations were rendered in watercolor.
Manufactured in China

10 9

The Library of Congress has cataloged the hardcover edition as follows:
Wright-Frierson, Virginia. A Desert Scrapbook: dawn to dusk in the Sonoran Desert
by Virginia-Wright Frierson.—1st ed. p. cm.
Summary: The author/artist describes many of the animals and plants and their
surroundings that she has sketched in the Sonoran Desert.
ISBN 978-0-689-80678-0 (h.c.)
1. Desert biology—Sonoran Desert—Juvenile literature. (1. Sonoran Desert. 2. Desert
animals. 3. Desert plants.) I. Title
QH104.5.S58W75 1996 95-19629 574.9791'7—dc20
ISBN 978-0-689-85055-4 (Aladdin pbk.)

1011 SCP

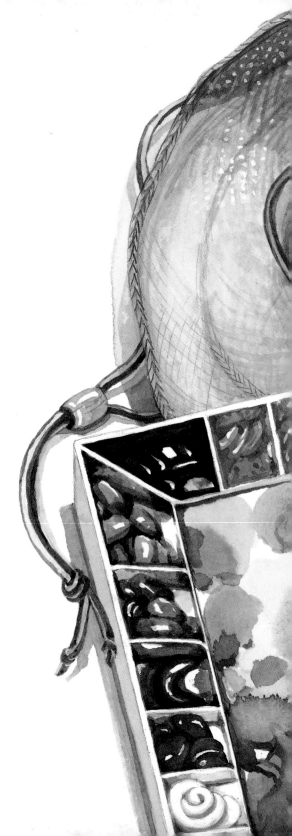

*For my husband, Dargan Frierson, whose work first brought us to the
Sonoran Desert, and to our Tucson friends who help us to come back.*

*The author would like to thank Ms. Carol Madeheim, Education Specialist II,
and Dr. Peter Siminski, Curator of Mammology and Ornithology at the
Arizona-Sonora Desert Museum.*

FOR INFORMATION ABOUT EFFORTS TO PRESERVE, EXHIBIT, AND
PROTECT THIS FRAGILE ECOSYSTEM, PLEASE CONTACT:

The Arizona-Sonora Desert Museum
2021 North Kinney Road
Tucson, AZ 85743

The sun is just coming up over the distant mountains. I pack up my painting gear: watercolors ☑ water bottle ☑ paper ☑ brush + pencil ☑ hat ☑ folding chair ☑ Now I must hurry outside to sketch some birds and animals while they are active in the cool early hours. This summer day promises to be another scorcher!

I find a beautiful view and sit quietly, listening and waiting for the animals to get used to my presence. Some people think that our Sonoran Desert is just a dry land of mountains, strange plants, and great sweeping skies. But look very carefully and you will also see many interesting creatures.

Once, on a spring day when I was out painting a prickly pear cactus, a desert tortoise crept up to nibble on a ripe fruit. I quickly sketched it until it crawled away with a red-stained mouth.

prickly pear blossom
- May

Another time when I was painting wildflowers, I noticed that a shadow kept passing over my white paper. When I looked up, I was surprised to see a vulture circling right above me. It was so close I could see its wrinkled head and the sunlight through its large wings. It flew off as soon as I waved my arms to show I was not dead and it would not be eating me for lunch.

Today, as I sketch some doves, I am startled by a roadrunner bursting from behind a nearby barrel cactus. It catches a zebra-tailed lizard and dashes off, leaving a little cloud of dust.

barrel cactus bloom - August
(my favorite cactus flower)

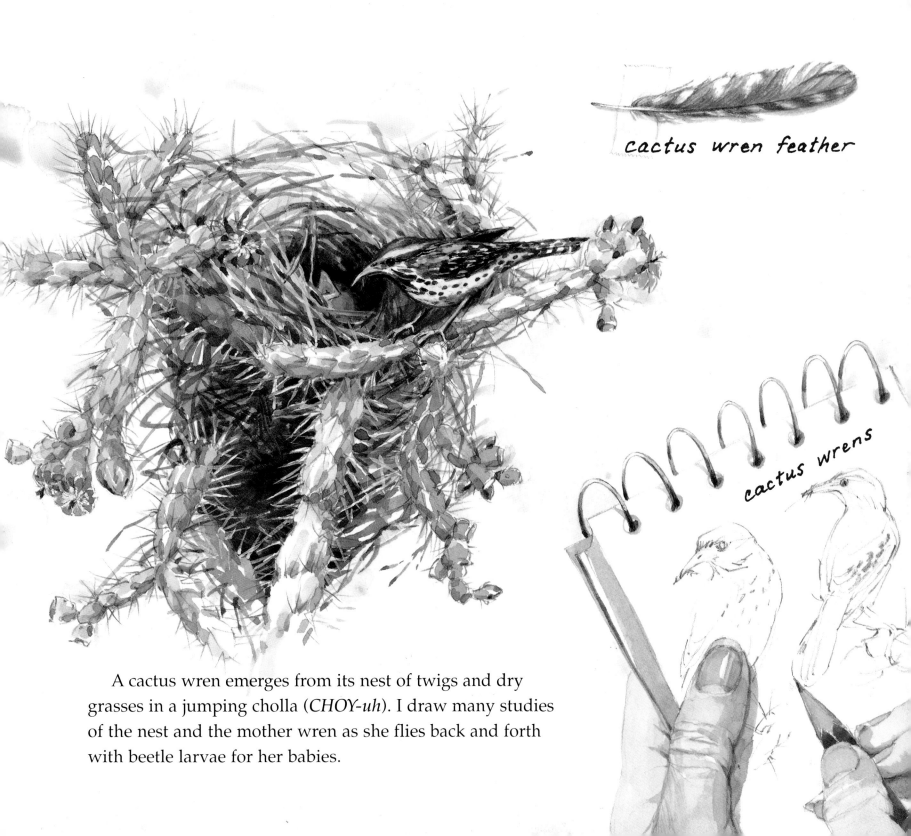

cactus wren feather

cactus wrens

A cactus wren emerges from its nest of twigs and dry grasses in a jumping cholla (*CHOY-uh*). I draw many studies of the nest and the mother wren as she flies back and forth with beetle larvae for her babies.

The sun is getting higher and the day is getting hotter. Most of the animals are now resting in cooler, shady places to escape the broiling heat. They will not come out until the cool of evening and the cover of darkness.

A tarantula waits until nightfall in its cool underground tunnel.

A desert pack rat is asleep, curled up deep inside its messy mound of cactus joints, sticks, leaves, bark, and rocks.

A desert scorpion hides under a rock, its babies clustered safely on its back.

A black-tailed jackrabbit rests in a shallow hole it has dug in the shade of a mesquite tree.

An elf owl sleeps in a hole in a saguaro.

A kangaroo rat lies asleep, curled up all day in its deep burrow. They never need to drink water, but get all the moisture they need from seeds and plants gathered at night.

A western diamondback rattlesnake stays cool in the abandoned hole of an antelope squirrel.

saguaro flowers - May

The creamy white flowers of the saguaros (*suh-WAHR-ohs*) have finished blooming for this year, and now the fruit begins to ripen. It is feasted upon by many desert animals, insects, and birds. This gila (*HEE-luh*) woodpecker has a nest in the hole it has pecked in the giant cactus.

*Gila woodpecker feather*

I rest in the shade of a palo verde tree and look at some seeds and pods I've collected. Above me, a curve-billed thrasher cools itself by widely opening its beak.

This small saguaro is about twenty-five years old!

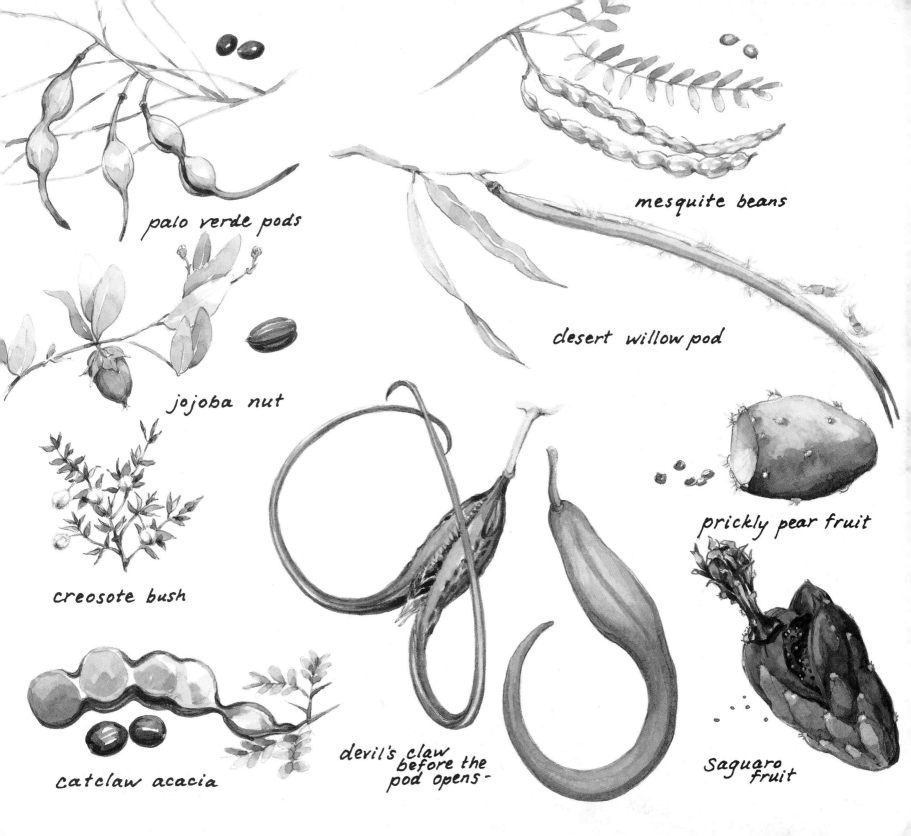

palo verde pods

mesquite beans

desert willow pod

jojoba nut

creosote bush

prickly pear fruit

catclaw acacia

devil's claw
before the
pod opens -

Saguaro
fruit

This story happened a few years ago: I was sitting on the hot ground painting a mountain view when I noticed a slight movement under a bush. My eyes focused on a huge rattlesnake, coiled and perfectly camouflaged next to my foot! I eased back, trembling, and as the snake slowly moved away, I saw a large lump in its middle. Luckily for me, it must have just eaten a cottontail.

Thunder grumbles in the distance and I notice the air is heavier. Maybe today will bring the first rain of the summer monsoons. The dry stalks of the ocotillo (*ah-ko-TEE-oh*) wave in the hot wind, welcoming the coming storm. I head for my home, looking down as I always do when I walk in the desert, careful not to brush against a spiny cactus or twist an ankle on the loose rock.

I drink a cool lemonade in my studio, which is in an old water tower at the house. The long-awaited rain begins to pour from the clouds, drenching the parched ground. The shallow roots of the saguaros drink up the precious moisture. The cacti will begin to swell with the water they must store through the long droughts.

With a great crashing of thunder, lightning strikes the tallest saguaro on the mountain!

It will collapse and its skeleton will stand with the wooden ribs reaching to the sky like fingers. But the fallen cactus will provide shelter and food for many insects and small animals.

I stay inside until the storm passes, carefully sorting some of the cactus spines I have collected.

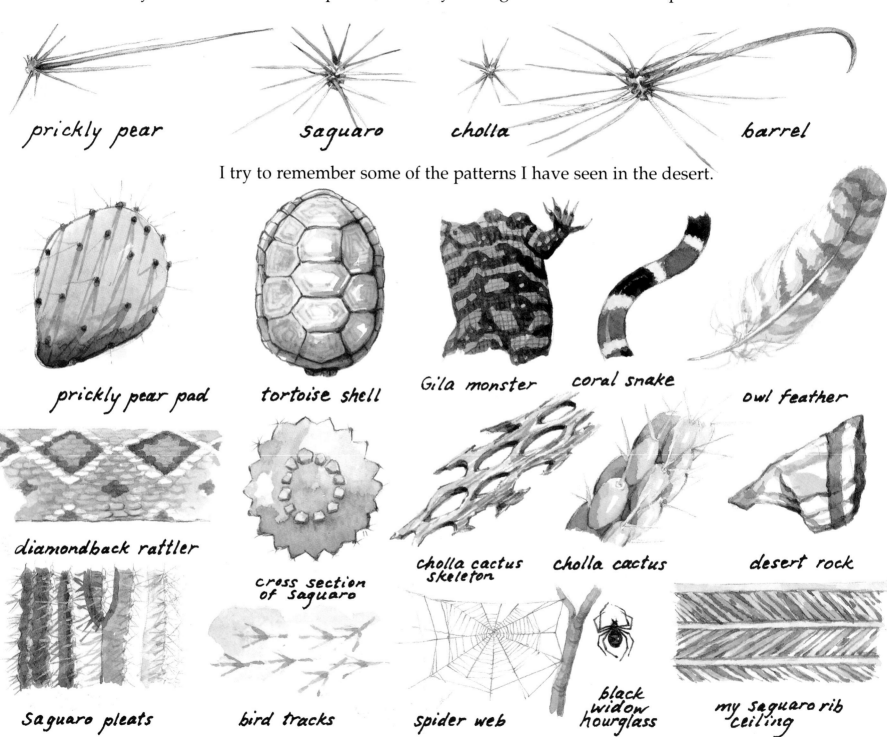

prickly pear

saguaro

cholla

barrel

I try to remember some of the patterns I have seen in the desert.

prickly pear pad

tortoise shell

Gila monster

coral snake

owl feather

diamondback rattler

cross section of saguaro

cholla cactus skeleton

cholla cactus

desert rock

Saguaro pleats

bird tracks

spider web

black widow hourglass

my saguaro rib ceiling

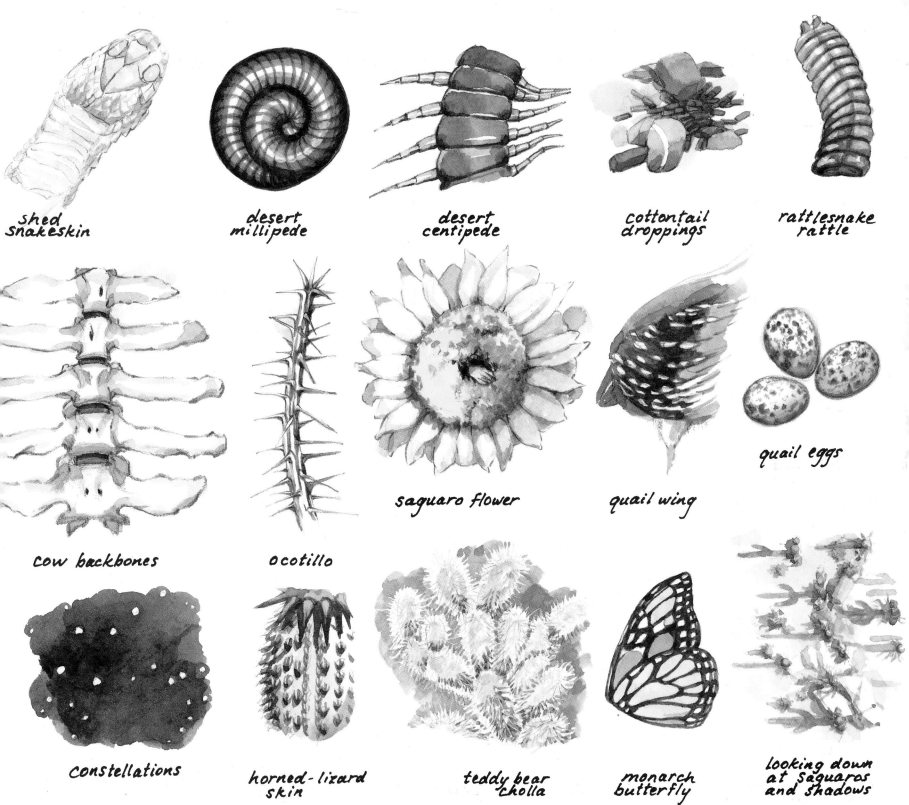

shed
snakeskin

desert
millipede

desert
centipede

cottontail
droppings

rattlesnake
rattle

cow backbones

ocotillo

saguaro flower

quail wing

quail eggs

constellations

horned-lizard
skin

teddy bear
cholla

monarch
butterfly

looking down
at saguaros
and shadows

I love to come outside right after a rain has freshened the air and settled the dust. I walk to the dry arroyo near my house and hear a roaring sound.

Suddenly, the arroyo is filled with churning water. So much rain falls in such a short time, it cannot all soak into the baked earth. The water collects in many streambeds in the mountains and becomes a muddy, roaring flash flood in the valleys. (Don't ever camp in an arroyo!)

By evening the spadefoot toads that have been buried deep underground all year have dug up to the surface. They croak and sing and lay eggs in the muddy pools. The eggs must develop into tadpoles, and then baby toads, before the puddles dry up in a few days.

The toads eat many insects in their few days aboveground. Then they dig back underground for almost a year to await another rainy season.

Once I saw several garter snakes feasting on spadefoot tadpoles in a puddle.

This group trampled all the tomato plants in my garden last night.

I sit unseen on the rocks and sketch a herd of javelinas (*have-uh-LEE-nuhs*) as they eat prickly pear pads and saguaro fruits. They leave a strong musky scent in the air and deep prints in the soft mud from their small hooves.

There is always a glorious sunset after a rainstorm. The pungent smell of the desert creosote bush perfumes the air. I sit on the rocks with my watercolors, trying to capture the warm glowing light and fiery colors.

The desert sky grows dark as I return home. A great
horned owl sweeps soundlessly above my head.

The air fills with sounds of life after night falls in the
desert. Nocturnal creatures creep out of their tunnels and
burrows. I hear an elf owl calling from its hole in a saguaro.
The toads croak and sing. Coyotes yip and howl.

In the studio, I spread out my sketches of these Sonoran Desert plants and animals, and the feathers, spines, and seeds I have found. I think maybe I will collect today's work into a scrapbook that will give a feeling of this desert day from dawn to dusk.

Javelinas

Outside my tower window, thousands of bright stars pierce the immense blackness of the beautiful night sky.

white-winged dove  antelope squirrel  desert cottontail  cactus wren  desert tortoise

tarantula hawk

black-vulture

harvester ants

roadrunner

bark scorpion

zebra-tailed lizard

pack rat

tarantula  kangaroo rat  black-tailed jack rabbit  Western diamondback rattlesnake  elf owl  gila woodpecker